N.H. Schenck

First Annual Report of the Chicago Young Men's Christian Association

Anatiposi

N.H. Schenck

First Annual Report of the Chicago Young Men's Christian Association

Reprint of the original.

1st Edition 2023 | ISBN: 978-3-38230-494-2

Anatiposi Verlag is an imprint of Outlook Verlagsgesellschaft mbH.

Verlag (Publisher): Outlook Verlag GmbH, Zeilweg 44, 60439 Frankfurt, Deutschland
Vertretungsberechtigt (Authorized to represent): E. Roepke, Zeilweg 44, 60439 Frankfurt, Deutschland
Druck (Print): Books on Demand GmbH, In de Tarpen 42, 22848 Norderstedt, Deutschland

FIRST ANNUAL REPORT

OF THE

CHICAGO

YOUNG MEN'S CHRISTIAN ASSOCIATION,

TOGETHER WITH THE

ADDRESS OF THE REV. N. H. SCHENCK,

CONSTITUTION, BY-LAWS,

LIST OF OFFICERS AND MEMBERS, STANDING COMMITTEES, ETC., ETC.

JUNE 20, 1859.

CHICAGO:

PUBLISHED FROM THE ROOMS OF THE ASSOCIATION,
METHODIST CHURCH BLOCK.

DUNLOP, SEWELL & SPALDING, PRINTERS, 145 LAKE STREET.

FIRST ANNUAL REPORT

OF THE

CHICAGO

YOUNG MEN'S CHRISTIAN ASSOCIATION,

TOGETHER WITH THE

ADDRESS OF THE REV. N. H. SCHENCK,

CONSTITUTION, BY-LAWS,

LIST OF OFFICERS AND MEMBERS, STANDING COMMITTEES, ETC., ETC.

JUNE 20, 1859.

CHICAGO:

PUBLISHED FROM THE ROOMS OF THE ASSOCIATION,
METHODIST CHURCH BLOCK.

DUNLOP, SEWELL & SPALDING, PRINTERS, 145 LAKE STREET.

OFFICERS

OF THE

CHICAGO YOUNG MEN'S CHRISTIAN ASSOCIATION,

Elected May, 1859.

————••————

PRESIDENT.

CYRUS BENTLEY,.............110 Dearborn st................First Baptist Church.

VICE PRESIDENTS.

R. J. RUNDELL, ...1 Masonic Temple,.............Baptist.
T. W. BRUCE, ...82 Van Buren street,............Congregational.
ROBT. II. HOW,.............51 Lake street,....................Episcopalian.
J. V. FARWELL, ...of Cooley & Farwell, ...Methodist.
E. D. HOWLAND,.............No. 4 Lind's Block, ...Dutch Reformed.
ALEX. BAINE,................cor. Carpenter & Hubbard sts.,...Reformed Presbyterian.
HENRY HOWLAND, ...of Howland & Co., ...Presbyterian,

RECORDING SECRETARY.

A. C. LECKIE, ...of Long & Leckie, ...13 LaSalle street.

CORRESPONDING SECRETARY.

H. D. PENFIELD,............with I. C. R. R. Co.,......... ...Land Department.

LIBRARIAN.

R. C. WATERMAN,..........Association Rooms, ...15 Church Block.

TREASURER.

L. E. ALEXANDER, ...Banker,............................Ogden's Building.

MANAGERS.

J. M. SPAFFORD,............85 South Water street,...........First Baptist.
LYMAN BRIDGES, ...with W. W. Boyington, ...Tabernacle Baptist.
WM. AITCHISON, Jr.,........with Underwood & Co.,..........Edina Place Baptist.
S. M. RANDOLPH,...........322 Fulton street,................Union Park Baptist.
J. ROGERSON, ...Elizabeth street, near Hubbard,..Berean Baptist.
J. T. GRIFFIN, ...with C. H. McCormick, ...North Baptist.
J. W. STANLEY, ...with Hinsdale & Babcock,........1st Congregational.
H. K. WALKER,..............with Marsh Bros.,..............Plymouth Congregational.
E. A. BOGUE,...............141 Lake street, ...N. England Congregational.
H. P. FISHER,...............44 Peoria street,.................Edwards Congregational.

E. F. SMITH,................278 South Clark street,...........First Evangelical Lutheran.
J. A. PARSONS, ...of Reynolds, Ely & Co., ...Trinity Episcopal.
J. F. ALDRICH, ...240 Market street, ...St. John's Episcopal.
H. S. NEWELL, ...St. James' Episcopal.
W. M. LUFF, ...with Beckwith & Merick,.........Holy Communion Episcopal.
H. J. BECKWITH,...Ascension Episcopal.
J. J. SPALDING, ...of Dunlop, Sewell & Spalding, ...First Methodist Episcopal.
A. L. SEWELL,..............   "   "   "   ...Indiana St. Meth. Epis.
W. H. RAND,................of Press & Tribune Co.,..........Wabash Ave. Meth. Epis.
B. T. VINCENT,..............with Vincent, Himrod & Co.,......Owen St. Meth. Epis.
SAMUEL DUNLOP, ...of Dunlop, Sewell & Spalding, ...Jefferson St. Meth. Epis.
THOS. WILTSEE, ...Sedgwick St. Meth. Epis.
W. W. CARR,................of A. G. Downs & Co.,...........First Presbyterian.
N. S. BOUTON, ...Clark Street, ...Second Presbyterian.
R. M. GUILFORD,...........with Reynolds, Ely & Co., ...Third Presbyterian
S. B. WILLIAMS, ...4 Pardee's Building, ...Olivet Presbyterian.
L. E. WHITCOMB,...........with T. B. Carter & Co.,.........Westminister Presbyterian
G. R. ECKLEY,..............7 Pomeroy's Building, ...North Presbyterian.
J. W. FARLIN,.............of Parsons & Farlin,...........South Presbyterian.
GEORGE STEWART,.........of G. & J. Stewart, ...Reformed Presbyterian.
C. S. HUTCHINS,............211 South Water street,.........Second Reformed Dutch.

STANDING COMMITTEES OF BOARD OF MANAGERS.

COMMITTEE ON LIBRARY.

E. D. HOWLAND, *Chairman,*

T. W. BRUCE,
GEORGE STEWART,
S. B. WILLIAMS,

J. F. ALDRICH,
THOS. WILTSEE,
J. T. GRIFFIN,

COMMITTEE ON FINANCE.

J. V. FARWELL, *Chairman.*

R. M. GUILFORD,
LYMAN BRIDGES,
GEO. R. ECKLEY,

J. A. PARSONS,
WM. AITCHISON, Jr.,
B. T. VINCENT,

COMMITTEE ON PRINTING AND PUBLISHING.

ROBT. H. HOW, *Chairman.*

W. H. RAND,
L. E. WHITCOMB,
J. M. SPAFFORD,

H. S. NEWELL,
A. L. SEWELL,
E. F. SMITH,

COMMITTEE ON LECTURES AND MEETINGS.

HENRY HOWLAND, *Chairman.*

J. W. STANLEY,
LYMAN BRIDGES,
J. V. FARWELL,

N. S. BOUTON,
L. E. ALEXANDER,
H. D. PENFIELD,

COMMITTEE ON ROOMS AND RECEPTION.

R. J. RUNDELL, *Chairman.*

W. M. LUFF,
H. K. WALKER,
W. W. CARR,

J. W. FARLIN.
S. M. RANDOLPH,
SAMUEL DUNLOP,

COMMITTEE ON STATISTICS.

ALEXANDER BAINE, *Chairman.*

E. A. BOGUE,
JOS. ROGERSON.
H. P. FISHER,

H. J. BECKWITH,
C. S. HUTCHINS,
J. J. SPALDING,

COMMITTEES OF THE ASSOCIATION.

Committee on Essays and Reviews.

WM. SCOTT DENNISTON, *Chairman.*

JOHN F. COOK,   W. H. MAGIE.
WM. C. GRANT,   LEROY SWORMSTED, Jr.

Committee to aid Strangers in selecting Places of Worship.

ROBERT BARRY, *Chairman.*

ALEX. JOHNSTON,   THOMAS FOSTER, Jr.
A. B. RUNDELL,   EDWARD ELY.

Committee to aid Members and Strangers in selecting Suitable Boarding Places.

H. B. HILL, *Chairman.*

THEODORE REESE.   H. J. WILLING,
N. B. RAPPELYE,   W. B. HOLBROOK,

Committee to aid Members and Strangers in procuring Places of Employment.

N. S. BOUTON, *Chairman.*

ASA D. HYDE,   JOHN BRODIE,
OTTO JEVNE,   WILLIAM RANDOLPH,

Committee to Visit the Sick Members of the Association and Strangers.

D. L. MOODY, *Chairman.*

JOHN GOEBEL,   THOMAS BEVAN, M. D.
D. A. COLTON, M. D.   GEORGE BRECK.

Committee on Devotional Meetings.

J. B. STILLSON, *Chairman.*

F. C. ROBINSON,   J. A. SCOVILLE,
J. S. L. SMITH,   A. H. CAMPBELL.

FIRST ANNIVERSARY.

The First Anniversary of the Chicago Young Men's Christian Association, was held at the Second Presbyterian Church, Wabash Avenue, corner of Washington Street, on Monday evening, June 20, 1859, at 8 o'clock.

Cyrus Bentley, Esq., president, in the chair.

The services consisted of a voluntary, by the choir of the church—"Rock of Ages."

Reading of the Scriptures, by Rev. William Krebs, of the Wabash Avenue Methodist Episcopal Church.

Prayer, by Rev. Professor Haven, of the Chicago Theological Seminary.

Singing, by the choir.

Reading of the Annual Report, by the President.

Address, by Rev. Noah Hunt Schenck, of Trinity Church.

Singing by the congregation—and the benediction, by Professor Haven.

The exercises commanded the close attention of a large audience, which dispersed well pleased with the first year's work of the Association.

FIRST ANNUAL REPORT

OF THE PRESIDENT OF THE

YOUNG MEN'S CHRISTIAN ASSOCIATION.

———◆———

The first year of the Young Men's Christian Association of Chicago, closes with the exercises of this evening; and the constitution devolves upon the President the duty of presenting at the annual meeting of the Association, a full report of its doings and progress during the past year.

In entering upon the discharge of this duty, I feel that I may ask my beloved brethren of the Association to join me in expressions of gratitude to God, in view of the many tokens of Divine favor which have attended us in this, our first year's effort as an Association. Truly, we have gained a name and a place among the philanthropic and religious enterprises of this city.

Many of us embarked in this enterprise, not without doubts and apprehensions as to the result. A few years before, a similar institution had arisen upon the waves of popular religious excitement. Hundreds of Christian young men gathered around, and sung loud pæans over the successful launch of the gallant barque, but in a few brief months, the storms of worldly care and business engagements blew over it, and it disappeared from the public view. And well might those identified with the first effort feel apprehensive as to the result of the second. Indeed many good Christian young men, whose counsels, sympathy and co-operation would have cheered our hopes, enlarged and strengthened our influence, and enabled us to achieve still greater results than without them we have been able to accomplish, so apprehensive as to the fate of our enterprise, have stood entirely aloof, apparently listening the live-long year for the heavy tramp of that procession, that should bear our remains to the quiet resting place of our deceased relative. But thanks be to God, that these solicitous brethren may to-night rejoice with us, that the Young Men's Christian Association of Chicago has withstood the storms of one year, at least. But this not of ourselves, but of Him who was our wisdom and strength, in the day of our ignorance and weakness. The Holy Spirit has been with us, encouraging our hearts and pervading our efforts, and with each revolving month, liberal accessions have been made to our numbers, and many young men drawn within the sphere of our influence. Nothing has been suffered to disturb the harmony that has uniformly prevailed throughout our entire membership, in our deliberations, discussions and labors. And amid the many bright and shining marks that have adorned the ranks of our soldiery, God in His good Providence, has suffered the shafts of death to be leveled at *not one*.

ORGANIZATION.

Prior to the organization of this Association, a few young men composing what was then called "The Chicago Young Men's Society for Religious Improvement," taking note of the flourishing condition of Young Men's Christian Associations in nearly all of the principal cities of the Union, resolved, notwithstanding the ugly precedent of the past, to make a second experiment of establishing such an Association here. They accordingly published a call, inviting all the Christian Young Men of the various Evangelical Churches of our city, favorable to the organization of such an Association, to meet at a specified time and place. This call was so generally and enthusiastically responded to, that steps were immediately taken, which resulted, in a few weeks, in a complete organization, adoption of a constitution, and election of a full corps of officers. These officers entered upon their duties on the third Monday of June, 1858.

The preamble to the Constitution, expresses in general terms the object of the Association, as follows :

"We, the subscribers, actuated by a desire to promote Evangelical Religion, and to stimulate vital piety among young men, resident in, or visiting this city or vicinity, and impressed with the importance of concentrated and united effort in accomplishing that object, and desirous of forming an association in which we may together labor for the great end proposed, hereby agree to adopt for our government the following Constitution."

The second section of the first article of the Constitution reiterates this design in more concise terms, as follows:—
"The object of this Association shall be the improvement of the spiritual, intellectual and social condition of young men, by the ways and means hereinafter designated."

By the provisions of the Constitution, four classes of membership constitute the Association—namely :

1. *Active* Members, comprising those who belong to some Evangelical Church.

2. *Associate*, comprising all who are elected on the grounds of good moral character, though they may not belong to any Church—both these classes paying into the Treasury an annual fee of Two Dollars.

3. *Life* Members, composed of all possessing the qualifications of either active or associate members, who contribute to the funds of the Association the sum of Twenty Dollars; which amount exempts them from any further taxation, and entitles them to all the privileges of the Association, unless it may be in certain cases, of voting and holding office, these being limited to Church members within the age of forty years ; and

4th. *Honorary* Members, comprising such as in the judgment of the Association may be worthy of an election to that distinction.

It is made the general duty of all the members of the Association, to seek out young men taking up their residence in Chicago and its vicinity, and endeavor to bring them under moral and religious influences, by aiding them in the selection of suitable boarding places and employment ; by introducing them to the members and privileges of the Association ; by securing their attendance at some place of public worship on the Sabbath, and by every means in their power, surrounding them with Christian influences.

MEMBERS.

At the commencement of the year, one hundred and forty young men had enrolled their names under the class of *Active*, nine under that of *Associate*, and two under that of *Life* membership—making at that time a total of one hundred and fifty-one members. Since then, the number of *Active* members has been increased to two hundred and ninety-three ; that of Associate to forty-eight, and that of Life to fourteen—making the present total number of members three hundred and fifty-five.

ROOMS.

During the greater part of the year the Association occupied a Hall on Randolph street, which, at the time it was secured, seemed the most available and eligible that could be obtained. It was leased until the first of April at a rent of Five Hundred Dollars per annum. Notwithstanding our efficient Committee on Rooms rendered this place of meeting in many respects, pleasant and attractive, nevertheless, there were insuperable objections to it as a reading and audience room, so that at the expiration of the lease a removal was made to the New Block of the Methodist Episcopal Church, on the corner of Clark and Washington Streets, a location unsurpassed in point of central advantages. In this new locality the same efficient committee have fitted up in the second story of the building, a large and commodious Reading Room, in a style simple and unostentatious, yet beautiful and attractive. There is diffused throughout the place, an air of neatness and comfort, well calculated to make the young man who resorts thither, feel more like being in the midst of the hallowed influences of home, than in any other place outside the domestic circle. This room is under the especial care of the Librarian, and some members of the Association are in attendance almost every evening to receive and welcome visitors. It is open from morning until ten o'clock at night each day, except the Sabbath, and all young men especially, together with such others as may please to come, are cordially invited to this pleasant retreat from the dusty arena of daily life, and to a free use of the Books, Periodicals and Newspapers there provided.

Besides the Reading Room, we have, in the next story above, a large and commodious hall, well furnished and lighted, where the regular meetings of the Association are held every third Monday evening of each month, and where the lectures before the Association are usually given.

Adjoining this hall, is also a pleasant room neatly furnished, where are held the meetings of the Board of Managers every second Monday evening of each month, and the regular prayer meeting of the Association, every Saturday evening of each week.

All of these rooms have been secured for the Association, at a less expense than the Hall in Randolph street, by one hundred and forty dollars, making our present rent three hundred and sixty dollars, which includes also the expense of fuel and lights in all the rooms except the Reading Room.

These rooms prove to be admirably adapted to our wants, and centres of attraction to the members of the Association.

LIBRARY.

As to our library, of course much cannot be said after an existence of but one year—and yet we are happy to state that a very good commencement has been made. We have to report at the present time, a collection of one hundred and forty-four volumes, all donated to the Association, as follows :

17 volumes by the Hon. Jas. H. Woodworth.
5 " by the Rev. J. Mason Ferris.
29 " by Mr. Wm. B. Keen.
1 " by S. C. Griggs & Co.
1 " by Mr. John V. Farwell.
1 " by Mr. J. H. Tomlinson, Jr.
15 " by the Rev. J. A. Wight.
75 " and a valuable book case, by the Young People's Christian Union of the First Baptist Church.

This collection, though small, is of sterling worth, and well calculated to foster a high-toned taste in the reading class of young men. It is our aim to provide a pure, healthful and religious literature for all who visit our Reading Room—and no book of unsound principles or doubtful morals finds a place upon our shelves.

While we are happy on this occasion to repeat our thanks to those of our citizens who have contributed thus to our library, we cannot but at the same time express our regrets that our variety of books is not more ample, and adequate to meet the wants of our young men, and that many of the excellent authors of the present as well as the past time, are not yet represented upon our shelves.

We trust however, that this deficiency will not long exist, but that the wise and good of our city, whose noble benefactions are ever responding to the apparent demands of our Saviour and His cause, will surround the nucleus of our library, with substantial testimonials of their appreciation of our labors in behalf of the young men of our city. We trust also, that the income of the Association, from the annual dues of the members, together with such fees of life membership and voluntary contributions to our general fund as we hope to obtain, will enable us to appropriate something

from the Treasury for this object. The necessary expenses
of furnishing rooms and getting an enterprise of this character into successful operation, have absorbed the means,
which, were it not for these, we should have been glad to
have devoted to the increase of our library.

NEWSPAPERS AND PERIODICALS.

Besides the books thus enumerated, we have in our Reading Room a collection of Quarterly Reviews, Magazines,
Weekly and Daily Newspapers, containing the latest news,
and some of the most interesting and profitable reading
matter of the present age. These are in part donated to the
Association, the balance are paid for at a cost of about $100
per annum. The papers consist of five daily and four
weekly, Chicago—two daily and five weekly, New York
City—one daily and three weekly, Boston—one daily and
one weekly, Philadelphia—one daily and one weekly, Balti-
more—one daily and one weekly, Detroit—one daily and
one weekly, Cincinnati—one Indianapolis, one Pittsburg,
one Nashville, and one Richmond, weekly—the Milwaukee
Sentinel; the New Orleans Delta, and the National Era.
The Periodicals consist of The American Merchant, a New
York monthly—the Presbyterian Expositor, and the West-
ern Churchman, Chicago, monthlies—the North-Western
Quarterly of Chicago—the Southern Baptist Review, a
Quarterly of Nashville—the Quarterly Reporter of Young
Men's Christian Associations, published by the Central
Committee—The Methodist Quarterly Review—the London
Review—the Westminster Review—the Edinburg Review—
Blackwood's Magazine and the North British Review.

MEETINGS.

The Association proper, has held during the past year,
twelve meetings, many of them largely attended and deeply
interesting. On these occasions various questions of Christian duty have been discussed with ability, with earnestness
and zeal, and yet, without exception, with decorum, Chris-

tian courtesy and a generous forbearance of each others views, to those of his brethren. At eight of these meetings essays prepared with much thought and labor, were read by eight members of the Association, respectively. The first by Mr. John E. Rhees; the second by Doctor D. A. Colton; the third by Mr. John V. Farwell; the fourth by Mr. L. E. Alexander; the fifth by Mr. E. D. Howland; the sixth by Mr. J. W. Stanley; the seventh by H. G. Spafford, Esq., and the eighth by Mr. B. Frank Jacobs.

The practical suggestions contained in these essays, and the cogency with which they were urged, were well calculated to stimulate and direct the labors of every Christian young man in the cause of His Master. And it is worthy of remark, that in no instance was the duty of preparing an essay devolved upon any member of the Association, but that the duty was promptly met and faithfully discharged.

Our able and efficient Board of Managers have also held their twelve regular meetings, and manifested their interest in the work committed to them, by a prompt attendance upon these meetings. The successful practical working of the Association, as well as the favorable financial report of the Treasurer at the close of the year, attests, without further comment, the wisdom of the Association in their election of this Board.

PRAYER MEETINGS.

Throughout the year, the Association has sustained at their rooms, without a single omission, a stated prayer meeting on every Saturday evening. The special object of which, was prayer for the young men of this city. These meetings have been spirited and earnest, and God has breathed in upon this circle of His faithful disciples, the influence of the Holy Spirit, and while our thoughts have recurred to many absent members of the Association, whose presence we should have been happy to have greeted, yet our room has been frequently filled with those who esteemed it alike their duty and privilege to thus assemble together, and pray God to speed His cause among the young men with whom we are associated in the daily walks of life. The unity that has prevailed at this meeting among brethren of different denominations, circled around a common altar of prayer, has been refreshing to all who have witnessed it, and seemed a foretaste of the joys of the world to come.

The latent spark of piety has here been kindled into holy fire—the weak in faith have here been made strong in the Lord—new fields of Christian toil and usefulness have here been opened up to view—and many a Christian young man, heretofore an inactive and unprofitable servant, has been inspired by the influence of these meetings to go forth upon errands of mercy, comforting the sick, feeding the hungry, clothing the naked, visiting the imprisoned and tendering the cup of salvation to those ready to perish. It would be of thrilling interest, had we the time, to narrate some facts connected with the labors of young men, who never knew anything of active Christian labor, until their connection with this Association. And we think it not too much to say that much of the impulse recently given to the cause of Mission Sabbath Schools in our city—that pre-eminently noble and Christian work—has been imparted by young men connected with this Association.

FIREMEN'S PRAYER MEETINGS.

Besides this stated prayer meeting on Saturday evening, this Association has also sustained during the winter, three prayer meetings each week among the Firemen of the city. One in Engine House No. 3, on the North side of the river—one in No. 5, on the West side, and one in No. 7, on the South side. These meetings, though shunned at first, have been many times largely attended by the Firemen, and were often occasions of deep interest to all present; and while we are unable to count perhaps, more than two hopeful conversions to God, eternity alone, can reveal the entire fruitage of this effort.

LECTURES.

Early in the year, the Board of Managers, through the Lecture Committee, made provision for a course of lectures, to be given mainly by the Clergymen of this city. Our invitations to these Reverend brethren, were all, with perhaps a single exception, promptly and cordially accepted. The course consisted of twelve lectures, delivered by the following named Clergymen, respectively:

Rev. N. H. Schenck, of the Trinity Episcopal Church,

Rev. N. L. Rice, of the North Presbyterian Church.

Rev. W. G. Howard, late of the First Baptist Church.

Rev. James Baume, late of the Clark Street Methodist Episcopal Church.

Rev. R. W. Patterson, of the Second Presbyterian Church.

Rev. J. Mason Ferris, of the Reformed Dutch Church.

Rev. Wm. H. Spencer, of the Westminster Presbyterian Church.

Rev. W. W. Everts, of Louisville, Kentucky.

Rev. J. W. Atterberry, of New Albany, Indiana.

Rev. Jas. E. Roy, of the Plymouth Congregational Church.

Rev. H. H. Morrell, of the Church of the Ascension.

Rev. Robert Patterson, of the Reformed Presbyterian Church.

We hesitate not to say, that this course of lectures transcended, in real merit, any course ever before given to the Chicago public; and were inexpressibly worthy of the audience of not only all members of the Association, but of all citizens. But so perverted has become the public taste for lectures at the present day, that a mere rhetorical flourish in the promulgation of infidel heresies, if made by a so called popular lecturer, draws the crowd, while the discussion of some great question of history, or of ethics, however superior in point of style and intrinsic merit, fails of hearers, if delivered by one dwelling among us. "A prophet is not without honor, save in his own country."

Besides this course of lectures, the Rev. Dr. Rice, at the solicitation of the Association and in aid of our finances, repeated at Metropolitan Hall, on the 14th of March, his able discourse in refutation of the prevailing error and delusion of the age—*Spiritualism*. Notwithstanding the extreme inclemency of the night, the proceeds of this lecture materially replenished our then depleted treasury. Likewise the Rev. Dr. Foster of the North-Western University, in compliance with the invitation of the Association, and in aid of our library, repeated in the audience room of the Clark Street Methodist Episcopal Church, on the 4th day of May, his able and valuable discourse on "Theodore Parker and his theology." The proceeds of this lecture are in the hands of the committee, and will, ere long be appropriated to the purchase of books for the library.

For all these lectures so generously given to the Association, without pecuniary compensation, the Association has by formal votes, returned their thanks; and we cordially improve this occasion in reiterating our gratitude to these brethren for the signal favors thus conferred upon the Association. May the blessing of God which maketh rich and addeth no sorrow, rest upon each of them.

We take this occasion also, to express our sincere thanks to the various newspapers of the city, for not only inserting notices of these lectures and of our meetings in their columns, but also for their liberal donation to the Association of copies of their papers. We trust this seeming sacrifice will only redound to a much greater circulation of their valued journals.

Our last lecture before the Association, was delivered at Metropolitan Hall, on the 21st day of April, by Rev. Henry Ward Beecher, whose presence among us was made available in two lectures, for the joint benefit of the Young Men's Association and Young Men's Christian Association.

In addition to these public meetings and lectures, a reunion or sociable was given by the Association at their rooms, on the 7th of February, not only to the members, but to the congregations of our various Churches, who were also invited to attend. This entertainment proved a success, and it is believed resulted in essential advantage to our enterprise. A thousand persons were estimated to be present, enjoying the festivities of the occasion. The evening passed most happily in making acquaintances, singing, listening to addresses from various gentlemen, all concluding with a bountiful collation served at the expense of the members of the Association, without infringing upon the Treasury.

COMMITTEES.

The work performed during the year by our various standing committees has not been as extensive and beneficial as we have desired. This is attributable in part, perhaps, to the difficulties always attendant upon new labors of this character—to a want of knowledge of the best mode of accomplishing the work, want of funds to expend in advertising, printing, and circulating cards, but still more perhaps, to the want of a willingness on the part of the committees to make personal sacrifices, and engage earnestly in labors to which they have been hitherto unaccustomed. And yet it should be mentioned, to the praise of many of the members of the committees, that they have discharged their duties nobly and well. This may be said of nearly, if not quite all, of the committees raised from the Board of Managers.

COMMITTEE ON ESSAYS AND REVIEWS.

The committee on Essays and Reviews, have also performed the duties assigned them, equal to our most sanguine expectations.

COMMITTEE TO AID MEMBERS AND STRANGERS IN SELECTING SUITABLE BOARDING PLACES.

The committee to aid members and strangers in selecting suitable boarding places, have as the result of much careful enquiry, prepared to a considerable extent, a list of boarding places, in which young men might find homes in Christian families, and thus be brought under such genial influences as would overcome any desire to associate with the dissipated and profane during their hours of leisure. Some young men have been directed to such families.

COMMITTEE TO AID MEMBERS AND STRANGERS IN PROCURING PLACES OF EMPLOYMENT.

The committee appointed to aid members and strangers in procuring places of employment, have accomplished but little. The past year has perhaps been unprecedented in the history of Chicago, for the difficulties attendant upon securing places of employment for young men. Owing to the extreme financial embarrassments that have prevailed among a large portion of our business community, a great number of young men have been thrown out of employment —and the demand for employees has almost entirely ceased. This difficulty has been so wide spread and insurmountable that the efforts of this committee have been almost paralyzed. We feel confident, however, that the importance of such a committee will yet be felt in our midst, and that great mutual benefits will interchange between employers and employees through such an agency.

Of course, it is not the business of an Association of this kind to furnish employment to young men, but rather to guard them against the evils incident to many situations in a large city like this—yet we shall gladly do what we can to point the honest and industrious to good homes among our business men, and at the same time prove ourselves an efficient agency in supplying the demands of our business community with young men worthy of confidence.

COMMITTEE ON ATTENDANCE UPON THE SICK.

The Committee on Attendance upon the Sick, in the early part of the autumn, divided the city into districts, each member taking one and distributing cards in omnibuses, hotels, boarding houses and other places of business, which read as follows :

YOUNG MEN'S CHRISTIAN ASSOCIATION.

To Proprietors of Hotels, Boarding Houses and others,

You are requested to give information to any member of the Committee of this Association for visiting the Sick, of any cases of sickness of young men, residing with you at any time, so that such attention as they may require may be extended to them.

These cards were signed by the members of the committee, and their residences noted thereon.

This committee visited a large number of persons in sickness, many of whom were heads of families, and rendered to nearly all both material and spiritual aid. They have stood by the bedside of the sick and dying, and patiently lingered at the couch of the young man, who without the restraining influences of Christian associations, and the counsels of pious friends, had plunged from steep to steep of dissipation, until debauch succeeding debauch had dethroned reason and reduced the man made in the image of God, to a level with the brutes.

FINANCES.

The reports of the Finance Committee and Treasurer disclose the following receipts and disbursements:

RECEIPTS—From donations in money, - - - - 234.95
    " Life memberships, - - 400.00
    " Proceeds of lectures of Dr. Rice and Henry
       Ward Beecher, - - - - 354.30
    " The annual dues of members, - - - 682.00
    " The sale of furniture, - . - - 120.00

      Making Total receipts of - - $1,791.25

DISBURSEMENTS—For fitting up and furnishing rooms, - $471.85
    " Rent of Rooms, - - - - 478.62
    " Salary of Librarian, - - - - 229.13
    " Fuel, - - - - - - 39.50
    " Gas, - - - - - - - 90.35
    " Newspapers, Periodicals and Postage, 100.00
    " Printing, - - - - - - 102.00
    " Stationery, - - - - - 22.95
    " Hymn books, etc. - - - - 10.00

      Making total disbursements, - - $1,544.40
      Leaving this day a balance in Treasury,
        with every debt paid, 246.85

                    $1791.25

So favorable a financial report proves the success of our enterprise and calls for the special thanks of the Association to their Financial Committee and Board of Managers.

CONCLUSION.

We have thus endeavored to present a record of the operations of our Association during the past year, and while it would have been our pleasure to have borne more welcome news, we feel to again thank God to-night that He has enabled us to make so successful a beginning.

And now, in conclusion, we have but to commend our Association to the favor of the Christian public.

Our object is to do good—to throw around the young man, whether a resident in our midst, or coming a stranger to our city, those influences that shall turn his steps from the snares laid for his feet throughout the highways and by-paths of our city, into the higher and serener walks of sobriety and religion. We seek his acquaintance, bring him into companionship with the wise and virtuous, and place before him the means of rational enjoyment, when, wearied with the labors of the day, lonely hours press heavily upon his spirit—and thus doing, seek to eventually make him a citizen of that city which is heavenly, whose builder and maker is God. Among our members, we strive to elevate the standard of piety, and stimulate the intelligent and the strong to more active religious duty and higher achievements of Christian labor.

Our organization is not intended, nor does it practically interfere with the denomination or the church. None of us undervalue the names by which we are respectively called, and believe that God suffers the diversities that at present exist among His people, that they may, by the variety of their service, the more effectually advance His cause. But all this does not prevent the association of different denominations upon a common platform of faith, in order that by the strength of their union, and the wisdom of their multitudinous counsels, the devices of our great spiritual enemy may be more successfully circumvented. Distinct and different in many of their views of religious truth, they harmonise in the great central Evangelical doctrine of Justification by faith in Christ alone. Like the cylinder, to borrow a figure I once heard employed, which has, drawn upon its circumference in separate and distinct sections, the various colors of the rainbow—presenting here isolated, and in bold contrast to the others, the Presbyterian's favorite blue—there the rubric red of the Episcopalian, and still further on the water color of the Baptist, and so on, when turned quickly by a single hand, presents nought but the purely glowing white. So Christians of different denominations, when moved by the arm of a common faith, symbolise that beautiful unity and harmony that will prevail by-and-bye, when we shall all see eye to eye. Neither do we hold to ours, as superior to, or independent of, but as auxiliary to the Church organization. We yield our regard to the Church to none. We remember that it is the most sacred of all fellowships, it being the Body of Christ—and rejoice that we are ourselves of its membership. At the same time we feel convinced that there are modes of operation in the advancement of Christ's cause, which it is not practicable, in the present condition of things for the Church as a separate organization, to adopt. And for the very reason that when we come together in our associated capacity, we leave all Church distinctions behind us, we can the more readily engage in those enterprises which if devolved upon the Church alone, might be hindered if not frustrated, by sectarian prejudices.

While the Church may be regarded as the regular soldiery of the Cross, marshaled under their respective pastors and teachers, may not the Young Men's Christian Associations constitute that flying artillery of Zion, ready at the summons of any and every Church, to fly hither and thither to repel the advancing wings of the common foe.

Let then the prayers, the sympathy and material aid of the pious and good be extended to our Association, and we trust that at the next anniversary we may present a still brighter record of gallant deeds done for the good of the young men of our city, and the glory of our Divine Master than at this time we have been able to do.

All of which is respectfully submitted.

C. BENTLEY,

President.

ABSTRACT OF AN ADDRESS

DELIVERED BEFORE THE YOUNG MEN'S CHRISTIAN ASSOCIATION OF CHICAGO,
AT THEIR FIRST ANNIVERSARY, BY

REV. NOAH HUNT SCHENCK.

It has rarely been my pleasure to listen to such a record of success as we have just been made to hear in the report of your President. The first year of the Young Men's Christian Association of Chicago has terminated, and exhibits at its close, rich harvests of heaven-blest effort. The annual report is replete with evidences of the faithfulness of your moral tillage. You have planted and watered well, and God has given abundant increase. You are permitted to enjoy the amplest testimony of the abiding presence of the Holy Spirit with you during your twelvemonth of associated labor. Your excellent President acknowledges, with the proper gratitude of a Christian and a philanthropist, that your society has been largely blest, and after recounting your labors and enumerating the different evangelizing appliances brought to bear in your varied work, ascribes to "Him from whom alone cometh our help," all that was wise in your counsels, efficient in your efforts, or blessed in your results. Uniting as I do in this ascription of honor to Him to whom alone it belongeth, I cannot go on and subscribe to the associated sentiment of your presiding officer, that this the "Lord's doing," is to be regarded as "marvellous in our eyes." The depressing influence of preceding failures, the general prostration of all commercial interests, linked as they are to all others, even those of an evangelical character, were as nothing when we come to remember the time when, and the circumstances, in the midst of which your Association had its birth. Bethink you how the waters

4

were troubled a year ago. Do you not remember the
thousands of sick and impotent folk who crowded around
the fountain of healing. Do you not remember how men
met and grasped hands and " spake often one with another"
about Christ, and the souls of their brethren. Do you not
remember the thousands who came together with earnest
hearts and tearful eyes, and anxious faces, day after day, in
Metropolitan Hall. You well remember that great natal
season of souls, when hundreds were born into the kingdom. You who had already "tasted the heavenly gift,"
knew what a " season of refreshing " that was from " the
presence of the Lord." You knew how every energy of
your moral man demanded an arena for its exercise. It was
then that the Young Men's Christian Association of Chicago
sprang into existence. Could it fail to be a success, fail to
enjoy the favoring smiles of Heaven. Thus rooted in a hot-
bed of grace, could this "tree of the Lord's own planting,"
fail to enter upon healthful life, or fail to bring forth fruit
speedily and abundantly, to the glory of God. The Christian energy which thus entered into the organism of this
society has ramified through, and been developed in every
department of its work. The report to which we have now
listened with such great satisfaction, is to be regarded as the
history of the adaptation of this energy to the spiritual needs
of this community, is a *catalogue raissonne* of the results of
this important gospel effort, is a picture of one of the most
precious of the fruits which we have been permitted to enjoy of the glorious revival of 1858. So let us look upon the
prosperity which has gilded the first year's history of this
society, as the legitimate product of the divinely ordained
means of grace, powerfully operating, rather than the result
of a dis-sociated manifestation of God's favor in its behalf.

Permit me, my Christian friends, to occupy the brief time
in which I may claim your attention this evening, with some
remarks upon *consecutive Christian effort*, as the one idea
which I deem most important for you to apprehend, and in-

corporate into the practical operations of your Association. In prosecuting the work you have undertaken, it behooves you, in view of the many hindrances to be encountered in the heart and in the world, not only to guard against every obstacle which the enemy may interpose, but lay earnest hold upon every aid to progress. These aids are to be recognized only by the light of certain great principles of life and action, of which you have sought to be advised by the divine oracle, which you have adopted in some hour of most solemn and prayerful self-consecration, and which you always bear about with you, as moulds in which to shape your thoughts, your feeling, and your work. The principle I now invite you to consider, is one which should enter into the code of every zealous laborer for Christ. It finds its truest exposition in the biographies of those philanthropists, who electing some line of evangelical effort have set their face like a flint toward the one object before them, "holding the beginning steadfast to the end." Its importance is negatively exhibited in the failure of those Christian enterprises which have been administered by an ever-changing sentiment and directed to the accomplishment of inharmonious, or at least widely differing ends. The plan of salvation, as set forth in Holy Scripture, teaches indirectly, it is true, yet very forcibly the value of this principle. There is a consecutiveness in gospel doctrine which even the "babe in Christ" is given to understand. Each one is linked to some other and in a defined and wisely arranged order. From the doctrine of "the Spirit's intervention," through the whole system, on to the doctrine of "Christly strength triumphant in man's last temptation," we are led to observe each principle of the gospel plan consequent upon some other, all interweaved in beautiful sequence, following the one upon another, according to a regimen conditioned upon God's love and man's infirmity, leading the soul from small to great, from strength to strength—from the first "principles of the doctrine of Christ," "on unto perfection." Permeating the whole of these are unchanging laws for the moral and physical man, obedience to which enables him to preserve in the practical adaptation of this doctrine a parallel to the consecutiveness observable in its theory. "Mortify the members," is the law of the body. "Submit yourselves to God" is the law of the mind. "Watch and pray" is the law of the heart. "Be not weary in well doing" is the law of the Spirit.— Thus in the reduction of doctrine to practice, the renewed man finds himself, for so long as he walks worthy his vocation, treading a path where duty is linked to duty and privilege to privilege, and joy to joy, in an unbroken chain from the place where he first turned his face toward Zion, even to the goal where his course being finished, he is permitted to enter into the joy of his Lord. Thus in the work, as in the plan of salvation, is our principle to be found dwelling and developed. Having this divine attestation to its importance, we may not be surprised when turning to the business walks of men, we find them practically recognizing its value as a condition of high success, and continually following its lead in the various departments of professional and trade life. *Singleness of purpose and pursuit* is inscribed over the portals of all the temples of mammon. It is taught by all the fame-bloated or gold-manacled oracles among men. It is a part of that system of practical wisdom, which faithfully acted out by "the children of this world" make them "wiser in their generation than the children of light," who are less regardful of its importance as a principle of Christian living. Those who are reclining on beds of ease in the high places of the world, will assure you that they achieved their position and gathered around them the purple and gilded trappings of honor and wealth by singleness of aim and steadiness of pursuit. Nay, all successful men will avow this as the controlling element in all their projects and all their labors. No less certain is it in its operation than the law of cause and effect. Just as sure is consecutiveness finally to attain the object toward which it is pointed.

These reflections prepare us in some measure for defining that adaptation of this principle to which I have already invited your attention. By consecutive Christian effort I mean *the concentration of all moral energy upon a specific evangelical work, and the persistent and steady engagement in this work until it be accomplished.* This involves, you perceive, the ideas of effort, of Christian effort, and of consecutive Christian effort. That Christian Church makes the best practical recognition of this law of a true evangelical life, which has the fewest changes in its administration, the rarest substitutions of moral discussions for faithful preaching, the most infrequent suspensions of gospel means for ceremonial or sacramental appliances. That individual Christian affords us the best illustration of this principle, who has adhered the most closely to the line of the Savior's precept and example, following after him the path of most manifest duty, and never diverging into the by-paths of experiment or compromise or mere moral procedure, who has lived with an "eye single to the glory of God" in the salvation of his own soul, whether "the working out" of that salvation involved only labor in his own behalf or labor for his brethren. That philanthropist acts out this principle most legitimately, who adopts, at the outset of his humanitarian career, a single line of beneficence for his life-journey, who prepares himself thoroughly for it in his closet and in his study, who enters upon it trusting unreservedly to the spirit's wisdom to guide him and Christ's strength to sustain him and God's favor to cheer him, who continues in it regardless of immediate results, neither dismayed by obstacles or inflated by successes, and who consummates his work in the same oneness of purpose and effort and submission to Christ as had marked its inception and continuance. But I behold in you, my Christian friends, an organized body of Christian philanthropists. You are supposed to have prepared for the labor you have undertaken to perform by much prayer. You have put on your armor and are ready for action, nay, have already spent a twelvemonth of active duty. I know your general spirit. I understand the principles under which you are associated. I know your field of labor. Permit me now to adapt this principle of consecutive Christian effort to the circumstances which environ you as members of this society; and as preparatory to such use of this principle, let me suggest:

1. That you resolve to live not in theories but in practices. One of the most fatal stumbling blocks to efficiency in organized bodies, is the common disposition to rely upon machinery, supposing that it is imbued with an *opus operatum* property; that if it be only cast in the right moulds and rightly put together, it will work of itself. That you fall not into this error, see to it that your "standing committees" are all *moving* committees, and that none of your members to whom you may delegate specific duty be permitted to "report progress" unless they give such detail of their labor as shall vindicate their character as true workers for Christ. And as a further guard against this error, let every member hold on to his individuality, never forgetting that as before God he is isolated, no matter how intimately his evangelical efforts may be united with those of others. Personal responsibility may never be ignored, may never be merged into associated responsibility. Though now you are working together, yet singly shall each one render his account. This thought distinctly held before the mind will serve not only as an incentive to persistent personal effort, but will give directness, and consecutiveness, and efficiency to your associated work.

2. Do not attempt too much. Map out your field, survey your resources and then stake out only so much ground as you shall deem proportioned to your ability as moral husbandmen, resolving that what you till you will till thoroughly, and spare no effort to have it produce the most abundant possible harvests.

3. Have no drones in the hive. I have no conception of the Christian, except as a working man, "working out his own salvation," and "never weary in well doing." Much less can I conceive of a member of an Association whose bond of union is labor for Christ, preserving a fellowship in "good standing," while his feet are in the stocks of inactivity, and his hands gloved with indifference, and his eyes shut to scenes of duty, and his ears closed to the appeals of beggared souls. Every one who enters such an Association as yours, is supposed to be seeking an arena for the exercise of the faculties of his spiritualized nature. Be sure that he finds it. There is work enough for all—work enough in this great city for ten times your number. It should be recognized as an obligation resting upon you in your aggregate capacity to provide fit employment for each of your members and utterly discountenance the notion of a "paying member" being exempted from any of the duties or responsibilities which devolve upon a "working member."

4. Seek wisdom and strength daily from God. "Praying always," is the most important piece of the armor of the Christian. The Spirit says, "without me ye can do nothing." I wish your weekly meeting for prayer might be a daily prayer meeting, as it has been in months that are past. But when you are not permitted to pray together, you can pray alone. Never forget the storehouse where all your supplies are garnered. The manna must each day be gathered. The soul will starve and its every faculty be palsied, except it have from heaven, each day, its "daily bread."

With these prefatory thoughts, I proceed to remark upon the adaptation of consecutive Christian effort to those who are the especial objects of your labor of love, viz: the young men of this city, and those who are soon to be its young men. Here we have two divisions of your proper work, the *conservative* and the *aggressive;* that which regards those who are already around you, your friends and acquaintances in the business and social walks of life; and that which regards those who are rapidly pressing on to take your places, the children and youth who are, or may be, gathered into Sunday Schools or other places for religious instruction.

1. We are brought then to address ourselves to the question, how can you make this principle of consecutive effort available to the moral preservation of the young men of this city? We at once observe that it admits of a very wide adaptation; but it is my present purpose only to speak of a single line of effort, and that which commends itself to my mind as most eminently practical, and most probably productive of immediate and lasting and beneficial results. Aside, then, from the general objects which you contemplate as a society, aside from your aggregate labor, aside from those Christian enterprises specified in your constitution and laws and embraced in your systematic operations, let me suggest to each member of this association that he cast about him until he finds some young man who is drifting a waif on the sea of temptation, and who, from the circumstances of his position, or from personal relations, seems to claim your individual exertion in his behalf. Thus let each of you select a soul for which you will undertake to make battle with the flesh, the world and the devil. Elect yourself its evangelist. Become its good genius. Arm yourself with the gospel crook and become its pastor. Let this one young man be the cynosure of your expressed religious life. Never approach the throne of grace without presenting there the circumstances of his case, and imploring the offices of the Spirit. Never permit a day to pass without some effort expended for the weal of his soul. See to it that he has the right books to read. Be careful to make provision for his leisure hours. Send him companions who will influence him for good. Make frequent engagements for him which will militate against his visiting places of great temptation. Enlist him in some benevolent enterprise. Seek, by all means, to develop his humanitarian element. Secure his

attendance at church regularly, and always at the same place
of worship. Do this on the basis of his duty to God if possible, or, failing this, do it on the basis of duty to society, or
as contributing to his personal success in life. Thus surround him with a moral atmosphere, and bring him into
association with things which are on the Lord's side. While
doing this, you must make him your friend, and be careful
so to order your action as to avoid any appearance of over-
zeal. Good sense, and a warm Christian heart, must be
your directing and impelling powers in this proposed work.
And this is not to be looked upon as the work of a week, a
month, a season or a year, not as a work demanding occa-
sional effort, not a work to be suspended after some little
disappointment, or some slight success, but as a consecutive
work, to be prosecuted with reference to the object you
have selected, no matter into what sinks of iniquity you
may have to follow him, no matter how protracted may be
the exertion necessary to effect any good result. You have
undertaken this business in a spirit which is not to be inflated
by successes, or disheartened by reverses, or wearied by
long continued effort, or broken by resistance or ingratitude,
or apparent utter failure. The young man you have as-
sumed to guide into the kingdom of Christ, or at least, save
from social ruin, may speedily respond to the appeals you
make, and be brought to stand upon solid ground; and thus
you be permitted to turn with like purposes and like results,
it may be, to another victim of sin's sweet intoxication; or
the first object of your beneficent effort may baffle every
attempt you make to cast his mind and heart in the moulds
of virtue, may, by his persistent pursuit of the baubles of
passion or fashion or fame, leave far behind the messenger of
"glad tidings" which you send after him, may be so forcibly
and rapidly drawn downward by the pleasing "baits of ill"
as to be insensible to any counter attraction. Either of these
experiences may be yours. It is not my design to picture
results. Neither would I have you make them the founda-

tion of such evangelical effort as I suggest. Rather decide upon such a line of action as this, because it seems to be a practical Christian work, which lies directly in the path of duty. Rather pursue it because you are convinced that it is a rational application of your Christian energy, and, while always hopeful of good results, never permit yourself to regard them as a condition of your patient continuance in this well-doing. If you only "plant" well, and "water" well, God will "give the increase." You may never see it, but you must have faith enough to believe it. "Sheaves," from the "precious seed," may never be garnered here by you, or in your sight, but, in the "great day of the Lord," men will rise up and call you blessed; if not those who have been the especial objects of your gospel labor, there will be others who shall have been indirectly, but inestimably benefitted by your efforts, and who shall be as "stars in your crown of rejoicing."

In mapping out before you such a field of action, I attempt to exhibit the principle of consecutive Christian effort reduced to practice and adapted to the circumstances which surround and the responsibilities which rest upon you as members of this association. I have denominated this your *consecutive* work because it is an effort to save young men *by* young men, to preserve to society and the church those who stand upon the same platform of age and occupation, with yourselves, and to whom you are allied by a thousand ties.

2. The other application which I have to propose of this principle, is in the line of what might be denominated your *aggressive* work and resolves itself into an enquiry as to the best method of bringing such Christian influences as you may wield, to bear upon those who are to succeed you, the young men of the next and succeeding generations. The adaptation of the principle of consecutive Christian effort to the work spread out before you in the Mission Sunday Schools of the city, is in my judgment, the best possible ex-

penditure of moral energy for the attainment of this end. The Sunday School, and especially the Mission Sunday School, presents a field which will repay with ample harvests the tillage you may bestow upon it. But this labor must be intelligently ordered, to produce such results. We are all constantly pained to hear reports of comparatively fruitless Sunday School work, fruitless because of the lack of persistent zeal in those who have engaged in it. Though every one must recognize " regularity" as the prime law of Sunday School life, yet because, it may be, that men regard it as so purely voluntary as to be an irresponsible work, they prosecute it in almost habitual disregard of this necessary condition of its success; and then, forsooth, marvel that so little good seems to result from their self-sacrificing toil for others. Such a zig-zag and broken line of procedure invariably confuses and finally disheartens him who enters upon it, to say nothing of the blighting effect produced by such treatment of the tender plants just budding with promise. There is a fearful responsibility attached to such a capricious moral husbandry—to this using the heart and mind of childhood as the mere playthings of a whimsical benevolence.

But he who keeps his eye on the compass of Christian duty will steer clear of such foundering rocks. To a thorough prosecution of your work as a teacher in the Mission Sunday School, the class you instruct should be one of your own gathering. You should go to the places, (so wretched are they, I can scarcely call them *homes*,) where the infant outcasts are, and where they dwell, as exiles from all good, social and moral influences. Familiarize yourselves with the circumstances of their domestic life, and convince them and their parents, that God has sent you to bear to them the gospel. Vindicate your earnestness by providing them decent clothing, and doing what you can to relieve their temporal wants. Then bring them from their retreats and marshal your little file of raw recruits in the body of the great

" Sunday School Army." Now your work is properly begun. The most rigid regularity in every thing is necessary to its successful prosecution. Aside from the direct results of such a course, there will be a thousand life-lessons indirectly taught by it. The continued lifting up of Christ to the eye of these little ones, (thus keeping the intellectual subordinated to the spiritual in all your teachings,) an invariable affectionate treatment, frequent visitings to enquire into the occasion of absence from class, or to supply some temporal want, the proffer of an active sympathy in every exigency of their domestic or school life, will soon weave ties of affection between you and your class,—ties by which you may lead them into paths of virtue and religion, and which will soon give you the sweetest assurances that your labor is not to be in vain, but that each truth imbibed, and each faculty developed by these little ones, are but so many tokens of better things for them and for you.

But this is not the end. Nay, you have now but succeeded in combining the elements of successful effort. That it be successful, it must be carried on as beneath a banner inscribed, "Never weary in well doing." Your class is your little christian family. Its members are your children in the Lord. As such they must be cared for and prayed for. As such they must be watched and warned. They must be always pursued by your eye of love wherever they go. Never be persuaded to give them up and form a new class. They will, after a few years, be old enough to organize themselves into a bible-class, and who so competent to teach them then, as he who has led them all the way along, from the hour when they received their first impression of God and his truth, the soul and its worth. By this time they will have learned to look to you as their teacher, counselor and sympathizer. By your advice they will be guided in seeking honorable employment. By your side in the house of God they will feel there is always a place for them.

Thus shall your consecutive Christian effort pluck precious souls from the sinks of iniquity abounding in our city, and surround them with blessed influences and fill them with precious truth, and prepare them for a life of faith, and so for an eternity of joy.

I have spoken of the Mission School, instead of the Parish School, because the former is the true type of a Sunday School, and because the latter may be left to the fostering care of those church organizations in which they are embraced. But upon the members of a Young Men's Christian Association the Mission Sunday School has especial claims. May I trust that you will never have a disposition to ignore them? Nay: from what you have already done, from what you are now doing, I know that you are alive to the importance of this arm of evangelization. As you further use it, may I beg you to systematize its action and ensure its efficiency by infusing into its muscle this strengthening, enduring, triumphing principle of consecutiveness.

Permit me to say, in concluding these hastily arranged remarks, that I regard the Young Men's Christian Association and the Mission Sunday School as the two most hopeful signs of the present age. They are marks of a living, not only, but of an on-moving church. They look to the occupancy of the sterile portions of the moral world and the tillage of ground which has always lain fallow. They are alike catholic in their character and compass, embracing in their organism and operation, true Christian unity. No better arenas than these for moral energy to wrestle with the powers of evil. No better theatres for the development and exercise of the faculties of our spiritual frame. No more attractive labor to him who would make full proof of his heirship as a son of God, and full payment of the debt he owes the brotherhood of souls of which he is a member. Go forth then, my Christian friends, to another year of Christian work, resolving that none of the evangelical appliances permitted you to use, shall suffer in your hands from want of a proper zeal, shall be inoperative because you have not intelligently or faithfully wielded them. Go forth, remembering that there are prizes in the moral world better worth the striving for than those which lie upon the altar of man's ambition; that there is a wealth of feeling greater and more enduring than any wealth of gold; that there is a glory in good actions more lustrous than crowns or chaplets, or any insignia of earthly office; that there is a heroism in active philanthropy both noble and ennobling, fraught with present blessing and pregnant with heavenly promise. "Therefore, be ye stedfast, unmovable, always abounding in the work of the Lord, forasmuch as ye know that your labor is not in vain in the Lord."

CONSTITUTION.

ARTICLE I.

NAME AND OBJECT.

SECTION 1.—The name of this Society shall be " THE YOUNG MEN'S CHRISTIAN ASSOCIATION OF CHICAGO."

SEC. 2.—The object of this Association shall be the improvement of the spiritual, intellectual and social condition of young men by the ways and means hereinafter designated.

ARTICLE II.

SECTION 1.—The members of his Association shall be of four classes, namely, Active, Associate, Life and Honorary.

SEC. 2.—Any male member of good standing in any Evangelical church, which holds the doctrine of justification by faith in Christ alone, may become an active member by the payment in advance of two dollars annually ; and if proposed for membership at any time during the current year after an annual meeting, said dues shall be estimated at fifty cents per quarter, till the next annual meeting.

Active members only shall have the right to vote, and those under forty years of age only shall be eligible to office.

SEC. 3.—Any man of good moral character may become an associate member by the payment of two dollars in advance annually, and if proposed for membership at any time during the current year after an annual meeting, said dues shall be estimated at fifty cents per quarter, till the next annual meeting, and shall be entitled to all the privileges of the Association, excepting those of voting and holding office.

SEC. 4.—Any man of good moral character may become a life member of this Association, by the payment, at any one time, of twenty dollars.

Life members shall be entitled to all the privileges of the Association, subject only to the provisions of section second, in reference to age and church membership.

SEC. 5.—Honorary members may be elected at any regular meeting of the Association, by a vote of not less than two thirds of the members present.

Sec. 6.—Any member of the Association may propose the name of a candidate for membership at any one of its regular meetings, but a vote shall not be taken thereon until the next stated meeting of the Association, when a vote of two thirds of the members present shall be required to elect said candidate.

ARTICLE III.

DUTIES OF MEMBERS.

Section 1.—The members of this Association shall seek out young men taking up their residence in Chicago and its vicinity, and endeavor to bring them under moral and religious influences, by aiding them in the selection of suitable boarding places and employment; by introducing them to the members and privileges of the Association; by securing their attendance at some place of worship on the Sabbath, and, by every means in their power, surrounding them with Christian influences.

Sec. 2.—The members of this Association shall exert themselves to interest the churches to which they respectively belong, in its object and welfare.

They shall labor to induce all suitable young men to connect themselves with this Association, and use all practicable means for increasing its membership, activity and usefulness.

ARTICLE. IV.

OFFICERS.

Section 1.—The officers of this Association shall consist of a President, one Vice-President from each denomination represented in the Association, who shall be chairman of the standing committees; a Recording Secretary, a Corresponding Secretary, a Librarian and a Treasurer; also a Board of Managers, consisting of one member from each church represented in the Association, and of which the officers elected shall be ex-officio members.

Sec. 2.—All of the above named officers shall be elected by ballot, on the third Monday evening in May of each year, and shall enter upon the duties of their office and shall hold the same one year from the first regular meeting in June following said election, and until their successors shall have entered upon the discharge of their duties.

ARTICLE V.

DUTIES OF OFFICERS.

Section 1.—It shall be the duty of the President to preside at all meetings of the Association and Board of Managers, and preserve in strict exercise the rules established by parliamentary usage, according to Cushing's Manual.

It shall also be the duty of the President to present, at the annual meeting of the Association, a full report of its doings and progress during the past year.

Sec. 2.—It shall be the duty of the Vice-Presidents to preside over the meetings of the Association in the absence of the President.

Sec. 3.—It shall be the duty of the Recording Secretary to attend all the meetings, and keep a correct record of the proceedings thereof, and notify all officers of their election.

He shall furnish the chairman of each committee that shall be appointed, a list of the members of said commitee, and a draft of the business committed.

Sec. 4.—The Corresponding Secretary shall, under the direction of the Board of Managers, be the organ of the Association in its communications with other societies and with the public; he shall keep copies of all letters written, and files of all received by him, relating to the affairs of the Association.

Sec. 5.—It shall be the duty of the Librarian to take charge of and keep in order all books, documents, and other movable property of the Association, keep a correct catalogue and account of the same, and also a record of the books delivered to the members of the Association ; keep a full and complete register of the name, denomination and church of each member of the Association ; also stating to which class of members he may belong, and an alphabetical index thereto ; also, a register of the names of persons proposed for membership at each meeting of the Association, which books shall be kept open, at the rooms of the Association, for the inspection of its members.

Sec. 6.—The Treasurer shall receive all monies due the Association, and shall pay all drafts drawn on him by the Board of Managers from funds in his hands not otherwise appropriated, and shall keep a full and correct account of his transactions, and report to the Board when required, and to the Association at its annual meeting, or whenever it shall be demanded by a vote of the Association.

Before entering on the duties of his office, he shall give bonds in the sum of two thousand dollars, for the faithful discharge of his trust, which bonds shall be approved by the Finance Committee of the Board of Managers.

Sec. 7.—The Board of Managers shall take general supervision of the affairs of the Association—its finances, correspondence, rooms, library, lectures, publications, etc., hold its meetings at least once a month, and construct by-laws for its own government: seven members shall constitute a quorum.

ARTICLE VI.

VACANCIES IN OFFICE.

In case of any vacancy occurring in any of the offices, the Board of Managers shall have power to fill the same, by and with the consent of the Association, until the next annual meeting.

ARTICLE VII.

MEETINGS.

Section 1.—There shall be a meeting of the Association on the third Monday evening of each month, for the proposal and election of members, for the promotion of social and Christian intercourse, and for the reception and consideration of such information as may advance the welfare of the Association.

Sec. 2.—There shall be an annual meeting of the Association on the third Monday evening in June of each year, at which time the reports of officers shall be read.

SEC. 3.—Special meetings of the Association, for the transaction of necessary business, may be called by the President, at the written request of five members.

SEC. 4.—Fifteen active members shall constitute a quorum.

SEC. 5.—All meetings of the Associations shall be opened by the reading of Scriptures and prayer, and closed by singing and prayer.

ARTICLE VIII.

DISCIPLINE.

SECTION 1.—In any case of immorality in any member of the Association, which shall be communicated in writing to the Board of Managers, they shall investigate it, and take such action, subject to confirmation by the Association, as may seem expedient; *provided* such member shall have the opportunity to make his defence before the Board and the Association.

SEC. 2.—In case of misconduct or neglect of duty on the part of any member, the majority of the Board of Managers may declare his office vacant; absence from three successive meetings, without sufficient excuse, shall be considered a neglect of duty. Due opportunity for defence shall be allowed the accused.

ARTICLE IX.

AMENDMENTS.

The provisions of this Constitution, by which none but members in good standing of Evangelical churches as afore-mentioned, may hold office, shall never be annulled; and no amendment of this Constitution shall be made, which would allow the said provisions to be annulled.

In other respects this Constitution may be altered or amended by a vote of two-thirds of the members present at any regular meeting of the Association; *provided* such alterations or amendments shall have been proposed at least one month previous.

BY-LAWS

Young Men's Christian Association,

OF CHICAGO.

ARTICLE I.

LIBRARY.

SECTION 1.—There shall be established, at the rooms of the Association, a library of bound volumes, periodicals and papers, selected under the care of the Board of Managers, which shall be open daily (Sundays excepted), from 8 o'clock A. M. until 10 P. M.

SEC. 2.—The Board of Managers shall have power to award to the Librarian such compensation as they may deem necessary and proper, in order to secure the constant attendance of himself or an assistant at the rooms of the Association.

ARTICLE II.

MEANS FOR EFFECTING THE OBJECTS OF THE ASSOCIATION.

SECTION 1.—Devotional exercises shall be held weekly, on Saturday evening, at each of which those present shall choose a leader for the next meeting.

SEC. 2.—At the regular monthly meetings of the Association, there shall be presented an essay, or review of some book, by a member of the Association, on a theme previously approved of by the Committee on Essays and Reviews, the reading of which shall be limited to fifteen minutes.

SEC. 3.—There shall be appointed, annually, the following Committees, viz:

1. A committee of five on essays and reviews, who shall select, at each monthly meeting, some member of the Association, with his consent, to read an essay or review at the next regular meeting.

2. A committee of five to aid strangers in selecting places of worship.

3. A committee of five to aid members and strangers in selecting suitable boarding houses.

4. A committee of five, to aid members and strangers in procuring employment.

5. A committee of five, to visit the sick members of the Association and such strangers as may be brought to their notice.

6. A committee of five, on devotional meetings.

SEC. 3. Except on special motion to the contrary, all committees shall be appointed by the presiding officer of the Association.

ARTICLE III.

RULES OF ORDER.

1. All regular meetings of the Association shall convene punctually as follows: From October to April, at 7 o'clock, and from April to October, at 8 o'clock, P. M.

2. No question shall be discussed involving points of doctrinal difference in Evangelical churches.

3. No member shall leave the room while another is speaking.

4. No member shall speak longer than five minutes, except when reading an essay or review, as heretofore provided, and not more than once on the same question, while any other member desires the floor.

ARTICLE IV.

ORDER OF EXERCISES AT THE REGULAR MEETINGS OF THE ASSOCIATION.

1. Reading of the Scriptures and prayer.
2. Reading the minutes of the preceding meeting.
3. Reports from the Board of Managers, in writing.
4. Reports from standing committees, in writing.
5. Reports from special committees, in writing.
6. Essay or Review.
7. Recess of fifteen minutes, for social intercourse.
8. Proposal of new members, in writing, which shall give name, class of membership, and if active, the Church connections of the parties proposed.
9. Unfinished business.
10. Miscellaneous business.
11. Singing and prayer.

ARTICLE V.

AMENDMENTS AND SUSPENSION OF BY-LAWS.

SECTION 1. These by-laws may be amended by a vote of two-thirds of the members present at any regular meeting, provided notice of the amendment proposed shall have been given at any previous regular meeting, or without notice, on the recommendation of the Board of Managers.

SEC. 2.—No objection being made, any by-law may be suspended during one meeting.

BY-LAWS OF THE BOARD OF MANAGERS.

ARTICLE I.

MEETINGS.

SECTION 1.—Regular meetings of the Board shall be held on the second Monday evening of every month, and special meetings whenever the President shall direct—in either case being announced to its members by circulars from the Recording Secretary.

SEC. 2.—All meetings shall be opened and closed with prayer.

SEC. 3.—Seven members shall constitute a quorum for the transaction of business, as provided by section seventh of article fifth, of the Constitution.

SEC. 4.—The following shall be the order of business:

1. Prayer.
2. Calling the Roll.
3. Reading the Minutes.
4. Unfinished Business.
5. Reports from regular committees.
6. Reports from special committees.
7. New business.
8. Prayer.

ARTICLE II.

COMMITTEES.

There shall be appointed by the President, at the regular meeting of the Association, on the third Monday evening of June, or as soon thereafter as is practicable, six standing committees, consisting severally of seven members.

1. Library Committee.
2. Committee on Finance.
3. Committee on Printing and Publishing.
4. Committee on Lectures and Meetings.
5. Committee on Rooms and Reception.
6. Committee on Statistics.

ARTICLE III.

DUTIES OF COMMITTEES.

SECTION 1.—The Library Committee shall use all suitable means for the increase and preservation of the Library, provide papers and periodicals for the reading room, and shall approve all publications previous to their admission into the library and reading room of the Association.

SEC. 2.—The Committee on Finance shall have the general supervision of the finances of the Association, and shall devise the means of raising the necessary funds for defraying its annual expenses. But no funds shall be paid out except upon bills presented to and approved by the Board of Managers, and for the payment of which drafts shall be drawn on the Treasurer, signed by the President and Recording Secretary.

SEC. 3.—The Committee on Printing and Publishing shall have the direction of the printing and publishing of all books, documents, reports, circulars and other matter issued by the Association, and shall attend to the distribution of the same as ordered by the Board. They shall also prepare and cause to be published in the newspapers of this city, such communications relative to the Association and its operations as may, from time to time, appear calculated to interest the Christian public in its behalf.

SEC. 4.—The Committee on Lectures and Meetings shall, under the direction of the Board, provide for the delivery of public lectures, upon subjects adapted to the spiritual and mental improvement of young men. They may procure teachers and lectures for any private classes that may be formed by the members. They shall also make arrangements and give notice of all public meetings of the Association.

SEC. 5.—The Committee on Rooms and Reception shall select (subject to the approval of the Board) suitable rooms for the use of the Association, and shall make provision for furnishing, lighting, warming and keeping the same in order, and shall do all in their power to make the rooms an attractive place of resort to the young men of this city.

SEC. 6.—The Committee on Statistics shall endeavor to ascertain how many young men are communicants in the several Evangelical churches in this city, the number of young men who attend divine service, and also the number of those who desecrate the Sabbath, and shall collect such other facts as may serve to show the moral and religious condition of young men in this city.

ARTICLE IV.

REPORTS OF STANDING COMMITTEES.

Each standing committee shall report every month, and whenever desired by the Board.

ARTICLE V.

AMENDMENTS.

These by-laws may be altered or amended by a vote of two-thirds of the members present at any regular meeting of the Board; *provided* notice of the proposed alteration or amendment, shall have been given at a previous regular meeting.

ACTIVE MEMBERS.

Aitchison, William, Jr.
Alexander, L. E.
Aldrich, James F.
Almini, Peter
Andrews, John S.
Annin, William
Baker, D. W.
Baine, Alexander
Barry, Robert
Barclay, J. S.
Baxter, T. W.
Benson, W. B.
Bevan, Thomas, M. D.
Beckwith, Henry J.
Bixby, Edmund
Bingham, S. R.
Bliss, Samuel
Bliss, S. S.
Blount, G. S.
Blount, J. H.
Bogue, E. A.
Bowen, George S.
Bouton, C. B.
Bouton, S. F.
Bond, L. L.
Bouton, N. S.
Bradley, F. E.
Brainard, J. S.
Breck, George
Bridges, Lyman
Brodie, John
Bruce, T. W.
Campbell, A. H.
Canfield, E. L. C.
Carr, Wm. W.
Chapman, J. E.
Childs, G. T.
Church, G. E.
Clark, Robert

Clark, Sumner,
Cook, J. F.
Carthill, John
Cobb, Henry M.
Coe, A. L.
Colton, D. A., M. D.
Couper, E
Curtis, P. W.
Drake, Frank
Darrow, G. W.
Davis, D. Eugene
Davis, Matthew W.
Davis, William J.
Deal, Geo. H.
Denniston, Wm. Scott, M. D.
Dennison, A. J.
Dodge, D. L.
Dorchester, W. H.
Downing, B. F.
Downs. A. G.
Doughty, W. M.
Dudley, H. W.
Dunlop, Samuel
Dunton, Geo. B.
Eckley, George R.
Eddy, Rev. T. M.
Ely, Edward
Ellis, Lathrop Stiles
Farlin, D. H.
Farlin, J. W.
Faircloth, L. E., M. D.
Farwell, Frank W.
Faulkner, Samuel
Ferris, Rev. J. Mason
Fisher, H. P.
Foster, Thomas, Jr.
Fox, Charles H.
Fuller, William
Funnell, E. W.

Gillett, Joseph F.
Goebel, John
Goodman, Edward
Goodman, James
Goodman, S. H.
Grant, Wm. C.
Griffin, Jas. T.
Guilford, R. M.
Gurney, T. T.
Halsey, Clinton S.
Harriott, Benjamin F.
Harris, W. D.
Hawley, W. D.
Hays, J. A.
Headstrom, E. L.
Heaford, W. H.
Hennegen, J. H.
Hesler, A.
Hernden, L. M.
Hickey, Rev. Yates
Hill, H. B.
How, Robert H.
Holbrook, W. B.
Hosmer, H. P.
Howland, E. D.
Hunt, S. M., Jr.
Huntington, M. J.
Hutchins, C. S.
Hyde, Asa D.
Jacobus, Oscar I.
Jacobs, B. F.
Jenks, W. M.
Jevne, Otto
Johnston, W. A.
Johnson, Geo. W.
Johnston, A.
Jones, D. L.
Jones, L. L.
Jordan, C. H.
Keegan, Frank
Kellogg, C. B.
Kennedy, S. M.
Kenney, Rev. Ira E.
Kerr, John S.
Knees, John L.
Lathrop, Rev. S. G.
Lamkin, J. B.
Lawrence, W.
Leekie, A. C.
Leiter, L. Z.

Lincolin, D. H.
Lippert, E. W.
Loomis, James M.
Luff, W. M.
Luff, Edmund
Lunt, Stephen P.
Lynd, B.
Magic, W. H.
Marsh, Thomas E.
Marshall, J. M.
Metlar, William
McDougall, A.
McLelland, Hugh
Miller, A. R.
Miller, Geo. H.
Mills, James H.
Moody, D. L.
Moody, Otis
Moore, George T.
Moorehouse, L. P
Morrison, John
Morrison, Daniel W.
Newell, H. S.
Nichols, John A.
Nichols, W. H.
Norton, C. A.
Officer, S. P.
Overy, John D.
Paige, Nathaniel,
Parsons, N. A.
Parsons J. E.
Parsons, James A.
Penfield, H. D.
Pope, George G.
Putnam, L. A.
Prouty, M. F.
Randerson, Thomas,
Randolph, Mahlon
Randolph, Smith M.
Randolph, William
Rappleye, N. B.
Raymond, E. D.
Reese, Theodore
Read, C. J.
Rice, Wm. H.
Robinson, Frank C.
Rogerson, Joseph
Rolf, J. A.
Roy, Rev. J. E.
Rundell, A. B.

Rundell, R. J.
Samson, A. B.
Sewell, Alfred L.
Scoville, J. A.
Skinner, H. R.
Sloan, T. J.
Smart, J. N.
Smith, Geo. B.
Smith, J. S. L.
Smith, Edwin F.
Smith, Frank B.
Spafford, H. G.
Spafford, J. N.
Spalding, J. J.
Stanley, John William
Steele, H. T.
Stewart, Rev. W. F.
Stewart, George
Stillson, Jerome B.
Stow, N. L.
Strong, G. C.
Swittey, Edward
Swormsted, Leroy, Jr.
Taintor, Charles M.
Taylor, E. B.
Temple, J. F.
Thompson, Theodore
Tomlinson, Wm.
Tomlinson, J. H., Jr.
Topliffe, W. B.
Tourtellott, W. F.
Trudeau, Charles,
Underwood, P. L.
Underwood, Sidney L.
Van Wyck, T. B.

Vanduzer, J. S.
Vernon, David
Vincent, B. T.
Wadsworth, Charles M.
Walker, H. K.
Walker, A.
Ward, Thomas W.
Warner, P. B.
Waterman, R. C.
Welch, H. H.
Wheeler, Wm. W.
Wheeler, W. E.
Whiteman, Geo. R.
Whitfield, Thomas
Whittle, W. P.
Whitcomb, L. E.
Whitehead, Edward J.
Wilcox, T.
Wiltsee, I. C.
Wiltsee, Thomas
Winton, D. B.
Winslow, W. A.
Wilder, E. C.
Williams, S. B.
Willing, H. J.
Wiswell, John C.
Wiswell, C. E.
Wilmarth, J. W.
Woodbridge, John
Woodworth, John Maynard
Wright, Andrew
Wright, A. M.
Wright, A. M.
Yale, John P.
Zimmerman, E.

ASSOCIATE MEMBERS.

Benson, W. B.
Blakeley, A. B.
Bowen, Chauncy,
Boyington, T. C.
Brown, James
Brown, David
Carver, B. F.
Chadwick, Walter
Cochrane, William
Davis, S. L.
Edwards, A. R.
Fisher, George
French, H. D.
Gerould, J. H.
Hallett, Moses
Heath, Monroe
Henderson, C. M.
Hogarth, James
Hurd, E. C.
Kemp, R. S.
Kent, Elmore A.

Lindslay, William
Lord, E. P.
Mason, J. J.
McDougall, H.
McWiliams, S.
Mill, James W.
Miller, John
Phelps, George P.
Potter, Charles B.
Richmond, W. E.
Shiverick, Thomas
Smith, A. H.
Smith, J. D.
Sollitt, John
Tweeddale, William
Warren, Robert
Waite, E. S.
West, J. C.
West, Wm. T.
Whitlock, Ogden
Wiswell, Agustus

LIFE MEMBERS.

Babcock, J. P.
Bentley, Cyrus
Bishop, Rev. N. H.
Blair, William
Boyd, Rev. Robert, A. M.
Boyington, W. W.
Burch, I. H.
Dickey, H. T.
Drake, Alexander
Farwell, J. V.
Fyfe, Alexander
Hinsdale, H. W.

Howard, Rev. W. G., D. D.
Howland, Henry
Hazleton, Geo. H.
King, Tuthill
King, H. W.
Lunt, Orrington
Page, Peter
Rand, Wm. H.
Ryan, Rev. Wm. M. D.
Stone, H. O.
Wadsworth, E. S.
Wells, E. S.

HONORARY MEMBERS.

Ferris, Rev. Isaac, D. D.